Also by Patrick Swenson

The Ultra Thin Man
The Ultra Big Sleep

SLIGHTLY RUBY

SLIGHTLY RUBY

PATRICK SWENSON

FAIRWOOD PRESS
Bonney Lake, WA

SLIGHTLY RUBY

A Fairwood Press Book
Copyright © 2016 by Patrick Swenson

Fairwood Press
21528 104th Street Ct E
Bonney Lake WA 98391

See all our titles at:
www.fairwoodpress.com

ISBN: 978-1-933846-64-4
First Fairwood Press edition: August 2016
Also available in an ebook edition.

Title inspired by *Slightly Scarlet,* a 1956 noir film
based on James M. Cain's novel *Love's Lovely Counterfeit*

Printed in the United States of America

This is for my friend Tod, who is actually one person in real life, not two.

Get that man some more Ranch dressing.

Someone had skewered the man's naked body onto the jagged end of a rotting post under Seattle's Pier 55. The old ferry terminal had been out of service since 2110, when folks started immigrating to the other seven worlds of the Union, so I didn't find it unusual that it had gone unnoticed.

This early in the morning, the pier was deserted, as it almost always was. The body, face up, dangled four feet off the ground, limbs splayed out as if prepared for some ritualistic sacrifice. It'd been impaled through the midsection, and large splinters gaped through his stomach.

I wondered when the unfortunate skewering happened, but Seattle Authority detective Shirley McCoy would have a better idea once the coroner arrived. I hadn't been part of Authority since I opened my private agency a few years back, but a morning run had brought me in contact with the deceased.

McCoy arrived just before nine o'clock and started examining the body jammed onto the post. She ignored me. She did that a lot these days. When she was my partner at Authority, things were better between us. Now, I rarely saw her. She talked to me, anyway, which was more than could be said for most of the department.

Three other Authority officials were casing the pier itself, top and bottom, looking for clues. I knew some of them. Amy Campbell, a crime scene specialist. Thomas Bloom and Ralph Sanderson, detectives. Neither of those two cared a shit about me. They were partners and had been for a long time. Sanderson saw me eyeing him and flipped me off, the son of a bitch. A few uniformed cops were there, too, most of whom I knew. Tom Charles, Michelle

Muller, Andrea Juangco. Muller took a moment to frown at me. So much love.

The water levels in Elliot Bay had diminished over the years, but the coming and going of the tide would have covered the body off and on, enough so that the skin would've had a slight blistering, patches turning greenish black. If the body had been through several months of constant submersion, and deeper underwater, the scavengers might have picked it to the bones. Birds had started to do a number on it, and some of them wheeled about the sky, keeping watch, but someone from Authority had generated sound to scare most of them away from the pier. The post had long ago splintered and rotted, and it had split into three spires. The body had been jammed onto one of the spires, and recently, but I suspected the man had been dead for longer than that.

It was late fall, cool and gray, but during the last few days, no rain had fallen.

"First glance, I'm guessing dead about

a week," I finally said to McCoy, "but here under the pier less than a day."

Her black hair bobbed on her back when she nodded. "Good guess, Crowell."

"I paid attention during the last impaling I investigated."

She turned and raised an eyebrow.

"Okay," I said, "not even."

She turned back to the body, focusing on the head. "Not something you see every day." She looked at me again. "Would a Helk do something like this?"

It was my turn to raise an eyebrow, and I added a bemused smirk. Sure, blame it on the aliens. "Only to other Helks, and only if they like them. It would take a lot of force to impale the body here, so it's possible a Helk could've done it."

"Possible."

"We've got a human corpse, not an alien one. A Helk First Clan wouldn't even fit under the pier. Not in this amount of space."

"So what do *you* think?"

At least I'd softened her up enough for her to ask my opinion. "Murder. We can rule out suicide."

"Brilliant. You can still call 'em, Crowell. Maybe your move to go private wasn't such a bad idea after all." She squinted at the corpse's head again. "Maybe you should slip away before the captain finds out you're here."

"He's still mad at me, huh?"

"A lot mad."

"Why shouldn't I be here? I found the body, so I reported it."

"Never mind. We've got something else going on here." McCoy pointed at the man.

I stepped to the side and took a closer look. The "something else" did not make itself known to me. "What am I looking at?"

"The fingertips," she said.

"What about them?"

"They're slightly red."

"Okay, I see. But not the rest of the body." I peered at the man's head, then his mouth, barely open, and saw something. I leaned in, hand outstretched.

"Don't touch anything, Dave."

I pulled a compact polymer spritzer from my pocket. So okay, fine. Maybe I'd acquired some extra spritzers during my time at Authority, and maybe McCoy wouldn't say anything. "Do you mind?" I asked McCoy.

"Just be careful."

I misted my left hand, waited a few seconds, and reached out again. Pressure from my fingers on his teeth pried the mouth wider.

"What in the wide Union is that?" McCoy asked.

Inside the man's mouth, a congealed mass of a slimy film coated the cavity. The substance was jellied, but as I wiggled my index finger in the mouth cavity, I knew it wasn't completely amorphous. The gunk gave way to semi-distinct shapes. There was a smell like rich, spicy food that had been left out of the refrigerator for days. I bit back bile.

The mass was mostly white and gray, but red splotched its surface, like visible capillaries. I wondered if it had something to do with the dead man's red complexion.

I pulled out one of the degraded shapes, and a viscous string of goo trailed after it.

McCoy put a hand to her face. "God, that's putrid."

"He may have been poisoned," I said.

"For those times when being shish-kabobed isn't enough."

I held the blob out to her. "Recognize it?"

She studied it, her face screwing up in disgust. "Not really. I can't get over that smell. It's like he had a craving for donuts and pastries and stuffed his face with them and died before he could wolf them down with something."

"Well, that's descriptive. Actually, it's that alien drug the Helks are experimenting with." I wiggled it at her, trying to get her to take it. "What's left of it, anyway."

"You mean RuBy?" She sprayed her hand with her own polymer spritzer.

"Yeah. But now it's showing up here on *Earth*." I held it closer to her.

The blob glistened as Shirley McCoy took it and held it between finger and thumb. "I don't know much about it."

"A prototype. Drug delivery through a coated paper of some sort. Nothing perfected, and it's dangerous as hell."

"This explains the red color in the goo, then."

McCoy returned the gunk to the victim's mouth and cleaned her hand on her black slacks. It reminded me to wipe my own hands clean.

"Here comes your partner," McCoy said, and she nodded behind me.

Alan Brindos dropped from the sea-wall and picked his way over the stumps and logs, his long beige overcoat trailing in the muck.

"I swear, I didn't call him," I said.

"Or ping him?"

"He'd just ignore it. Honestly, he would prefer doing something else. Says we should close the agency, take the money, and run."

"You've made money doing this?"

"Okay, just run."

"Like that will help."

"Okay, just close the agency."

"Now you're talking."

"But I do like to eat."

"And you need money to do that."

"I could always sneak food out of the Authority Commissary. The cafeteria staff still loves me."

Brindos stumbled slightly as he came up to us, grunted something that might've been a hello, then made a beeline to the body.

McCoy held out her arm. "Brindos, don't—"

"I know who he is." Brindos did what McCoy hadn't wanted him to do and put his hand on the man's chest. It seemed almost a sympathetic gesture.

I nudged his elbow, trying to get him to look at me. "Who is he?"

"And more importantly," McCoy said, "how did you know he was here?"

"He listened to the police scanners," I said.

"The what?"

"Never mind."

"Don't give me your nostalgic bullshit, Crowell," she said.

Brindos finally turned from the body. "He called."

I waved my hand in McCoy's direction. "I swear, I *didn't*."

"Not you, Dave. Him." Brindos pointed at our victim. "*He* called."

"Before all this happened?" I asked.

Brindos didn't answer.

McCoy stuffed her hands into her pockets. "Who is he?"

"His name is Brenden Thorne," Brindos said. "He's the vice president of customer relations for TWT."

"Transworld Transport," I muttered.

"Worlds Apart," Brindos said, quoting the TWT catchphrase.

And committed to Union.

"And he called . . . why?"

Brindos dug in his coat pocket. "He knew about our agency. He found our info on the DataNet, called, and hired us."

"*Hired* us? When?"

"An hour ago."

"An hour—" I stopped to let my brain catch up. It sometimes liked to lag behind. "He's been dead at least a week."

Brindos held out his comm card, its flashpaper surface dark, the skin of it unexpanded. "Unregistered ping, on the voice node, a scheduled delay, delivered an hour ago."

"So he knew he was going to be murdered?" McCoy asked. She blinked at the dead man.

"Apparently so," Brindos said. "And he paid up front."

I frowned, pulled out my own comm card, and found the DataNet node. A brief moment passed as I whispered my finger to the agency account. I expanded the flash-paper, pulling the display larger and away from the card. Most comm cards couldn't do all of this, but Brindos was a master at tinkering with the tech.

A moment later, I had confirmation. "Large deposit in my account. Enough for two jobs."

Brindos put a hand on the man's chest again. "Or one extremely dangerous job."

"What else did he say?"

Brindos didn't hesitate. "He said, 'Solve my murder.'"

I looked at him. Then I looked at McCoy. She looked at me. Then she looked at Brindos, and Brindos looked at Brenden Thorne.

McCoy said, "Holy shit."

"That's it?" I asked. "Solve my murder, and nothing else?"

Brindos pulled away from the body and walked past me, retracing his steps back to the seawall.

"He said nothing else?" I yelled at him. "Where the hell are you *going*?"

"I'm getting to work on this case."

"Alan. It's murder. It's Authority's case."

"He hired us."

"What *else* did he say?"

Brindos stopped, turned, and stared us down. "He told us the name of the man who murdered him." He waited a few seconds to let that sink in, then continued on his way to the seawall.

I blinked and watched his retreating overcoat.

Barely audible beside me, Shirley Mc-Coy said again, "Holy shit."

"Yeah."

"Just . . . go with him. Get the name, and let me know, will you?"

I nodded, but said nothing.

McCoy whispered, "He named his murderer."

I stared at Brenden Thorne, the dead man savagely dispatched on a broken pier post. "So it'll be easy then."

Shirley McCoy did not offer me a ride back to my office up James Street, at the 7th Street Apartments. The lower level had converted to low-rent office space three years back when rent prices in the downtown area dropped. It'd been an easy jaunt *down* the hill to the waterfront, but it took a more concerted effort to trudge back up, particularly when I didn't feel like finishing my run.

Alan Brindos lounged in the chair behind my desk when I slid confidently through the apartment door, pretending I didn't ache from the hill climb. The heavy breathing gave me away.

I didn't ask how *he'd* got back.

"John Grosko," Brindos said, "a Third Clan Helk."

Leaning on the desk with my balled fists, I tried to catch my breath. John Grosko, the name of the man who murdered Brenden Thorne. "Human first name, Helk surname."

"Snot for brains, I'm sure." Brindos—lean and good looking, younger than me by ten years, barely old enough for this kind of work—had a cynical streak a mile long.

"So who's John Grosko?" I asked.

"A ghost."

"A what?"

"He's dead."

I knew there'd be a catch. "A dead man tells us he was killed by a dead man."

"Isn't this fun."

"So who's John Grosko?" I repeated.

"DataNet has little. A minor run-in with Earth Authority when he showed up here last month. Brought in for drug dealing, but nothing stuck or led to his incarceration. They let him go."

Drugs. A connection to the dissolved RuBy in Thorne's mouth, perhaps. But if

RuBy was the drug, someone would've reported it. "He was on Earth when he died?"

Brindos nodded.

"And how did he die?"

"Unknown. They found the body on a farm, and the coroner hadn't performed the autopsy."

"But let me guess. Grosko was dead before our victim."

"By several days," Brindos said, "if Thorne was indeed dead for a week."

"And there's a body? Confirmation of one?"

"A report that he ended up in the morgue. But—"

"The body went missing."

He stood and nodded at me to take the chair. I didn't object. John Grosko's file flickered on the DataNet terminal. The Helk's leathery head filled the screen, his smile showing sharp teeth, ragged and dirty. Pretty as a picture, these Helks. Grosko's particulars scrolled in a loop down the left side. The DataNet was good, but I couldn't access the full Authority report on him.

"He worked for Abigail Graff," I said, spotting the name and the connection. She was human, a known criminal from Chicago, and after an incident that caught the attention of the NIO, she fell onto a Union watch list.

"Who's Abigail Graff?" Brindos asked. He slumped into the client chair. The walls rattled a moment as the water pipes struggled to work for someone on the upper floors.

"A thug from Chicago, but she's traveled back and forth between here and Helkunntanas."

"Let me guess," Brindos said. "Via Transworld Transport."

I reconfigured the DataNet protocols and whisked my finger along a node Brindos had programmed to open a back door into the DataNet Basement. He'd done this sort of illegally, but this is why I kept Alan Brindos around. He was good at being illegal without getting caught.

"Graff is connected to Brenden Thorne all right," I said. "Solid history of TWT donations to a non-disclosed dye-works in the Swain district on Helkunntanas. Same district Graff's been to fairly regularly."

"Doing what?"

The DataNet pinged me with an informational node from Seattle Authority. McCoy. Why wasn't she pinging my comm card instead of my DataNet terminal? I liked holdover, outdated tech, but the damn terminals were clunky at best.

I said, "Good question."

"Of course it's good. Do we find Graff then? Is she here or on Helkunntanas?"

I responded to McCoy's ping, a request for the murderer's name. She'd thought I'd forgotten. I sent the name, and asked her to meet me in half an hour at Zola's, a café a few blocks from my office. I knew she'd say yes, and I didn't even look at the response.

"I think our time would be better served looking for John Grosko." I closed down the DataNet and eyed the office bathroom, anxious to clean up after my morning run.

"The dead guy," Brindos said. "You want to find the dead guy."

"He's the one Thorne named, so we find him, dead or not." I rose from my chair, and Brindos stood and stopped me with a hand on my arm.

"What'd you just find on the Net?" he asked.

"A clue."

"What clue?"

"Shirley McCoy."

"She's a clue?"

"She's going to give me one when she looks up John Grosko."

"Because?"

I patted Brindos's hand and he let go of my arm. "She was the arresting officer when John Grosko was brought in for drug dealing."

Zola's isn't so much a café as a hangout for data-heads and down-on-their-luck locals looking for an hour free with the café's immersion specs. With food or drink purchase, of course. That's entertainment.

I arrived right on time. I'd showered, then dressed in the black slacks and gray button-down shirt I'd worn to work. In my rush to get to Zola's, I couldn't find my jacket, so I had my blaster tucked in my waistband, my shirt covering it. I was a bit cold.

Shirley McCoy was already seated at my favorite table in the back corner. After years working together, she knew it was my favorite. As I approached, she slapped her comm card, the flashpaper display shrinking and sinking back out of sight into the plastic. She wore a coat as gray as the Seattle sky. A red scarf hung loose around her neck. On the table next to her, half empty, was a glass of Temonus whiskey, its blue color reflecting in the glass.

Only a few other patrons sat at the tables. They were all immersed in their immersion specs.

I sat down and waved for our server. No servo-bots here, of course. Tod, a young kid who'd served me before, came over and took my order for a coffee and fries. He wore a Zola's staff T-shirt and a holo nametag that alternated between the café's logo and his name.

"Just fries?" McCoy asked. "I hope that's not your lunch."

I pointed at the whiskey. "I hope that's not yours."

"John Grosko."

Right to the point. "You arrested him last year. Is he really dead?"

She took a sip of the whiskey. "We

think so. How solid is your information from Brenden Thorne that Grosko is his killer?"

"As solid as you'd expect coming from a dead man. So what do you have on Grosko?"

"Like you mentioned in your ping, he has ties to Abigail Graff. Graff is squeaky clean, but Grosko has a history of trips through the jump slot to and from Helkunntanas. There's a payment trail to Grosko from TWT that didn't come up in a surface DataNet search, so it's very possible Brenden Thorne was involved in a scheme to get the Helk from place to place quietly."

"Is it coincidence he's the Customer Relations VP?"

"Don't know. But if he's involved, it definitely turned sour."

More than that, it turned red. The drug, RuBy, packed into Brenden Thorne's throat, choking him, or poisoning him, or both. So much for customer relations.

I mulled it over. So did McCoy as she sipped her whiskey. Tod brought my coffee and I sipped it. We mulled things over some more without talking. My fries came. They were cold, and I sent them back.

"What else can you tell me?" I asked.

She rotated her whiskey glass a full 360 before answering. "The official investigation is underway, of course. Lots of Authority down at the crime scene."

"I mean about Grosko."

She reached into her coat pocket and came out with a virt tab. Barely visible on the tab's slick surface, the letters s.a. labeled it as property of Seattle Authority. "My files on Grosko, from the arrest." She handed it to me. "Maybe you'll find something I didn't."

"Captain Santos know you're giving this to me?"

"What do you think?"

I turned the tab over a few times with fingers and thumb. "Thanks, Shirl, I appreciate it."

"What're friends for?"

"I can make a list."

She downed the last of the whiskey and stood. "Gotta get back."

"But my fries are just getting here." Tod worked his way to me with a platter. Steam rose from it, so at least the fries were hot. He placed them before me and apologized awkwardly for the wait. I nodded, and he disappeared into the kitchen.

McCoy stole a fry from the platter and waved it at me. "Keep me posted, you hear?" She folded it into her mouth, tapped me on the shoulder, and left Zola's without another word.

Short and sweet. That was Shirley McCoy. Actually, that was most of Authority these days. They had a shortage of cops and plenty to do, even on a world with rapidly depopulating cities. The more serious cases either wrapped up fast, or disappeared into cold storage, unsolved. McCoy had solved her fair share of them, and filed away others. Captain Monte Santos worked her to the bone, fleshed her out again with frequent promotions, dressed her up with connections to politicians and business leaders, and put her right back to work. Santos liked her.

Lately, she'd been working without a partner. If I hadn't left for private work and abandoned Santos's favorite cop during the summer when Authority actually had more cases than they could handle, Santos might still like me too. To help me out, I hired Alan Brindos, a young man with a less than stellar reputation with Authority, and that hadn't helped matters.

At least this new case would get me caught up on some of the agency's bills. This is why I was here at Zola's eating French fries instead of joining Shirley Mc-Coy at the mayor's fundraiser dinners.

Tod came back out of the kitchen, and I waved him down.

"These fries could use some Ranch dressing."

As I was about to leave, Zola's wall screen showed the press coverage of the murder. I stopped to watch. The anchor desk tossed it to a reporter near the pier, who was as close to the scene as he could get, but not near enough to show any details. He reported what he knew, which turned out to be more than I expected him to know: an unidentified male under the pier, a brutal killing, horrendous chest wounds, and drug-related. I didn't stick around to watch more.

I walked back toward the office building, fingering McCoy's virt tab in my pocket. The sky was still the color of McCoy's coat. It was still cold. When I arrived at the office building, Brindos stood on the sidewalk in front of the doorway. He didn't seem to be doing anything except staring at the other side of the street.

"What're you doing?" I asked.

"A stake-out."

"Shouldn't you be in a vehicle to do that?"

He pointed across the street at a ground car parked at an angle, its chassis flush to the ground, its repulsors off, the engine off. Two men sat in the front seat, looking our way.

"See?" I held up my hands. "*They* know you need to be in a vehicle."

Brindos grunted. "But they don't know they're supposed to be stealthy."

"I could wave to them."

"I think they're waiting for you."

"Mr. Popular."

He sniffed. "You smell like French fries."

"This is why I keep you around, Master Sleuth. C'mon, don't worry about them." I walked past him to the door.

Once inside the office, I closed the

door. If the two men were going to make a run at us, it would be sooner than later, and why not let them face a closed door? I positioned myself in front of my desk. Brindos stood near two old filing cabinets. Not many files in there.

I couldn't see the street from my office, so I didn't know if the ground car was still there. I was just wondering if I should go out and check on them when the two men came in through the door without knocking, looking formidable. They were both big, wide men, bundled in black coats cinched around their necks. They wore black slacks and brown shoes. One had brown hair, medium-length, parted down the middle, and the other was bald. Young, cocky, inexperienced. Like they thought size was all the intimidation they needed.

I wasn't sure either of them had weapons, blaster or otherwise. They looked confident, and I figured they wanted to use their bulk against us.

"Gentlemen," I said, my hands on my hips, my blaster within easy reach tucked in my pants' waistband, hidden under my shirt. "Have you lost something that needs finding? Or are you just lost?"

"Shut up," the bald man said. He nodded at Brindos, and the brown-haired man took two steps toward him and tried to look menacing, his hands twitching slightly at his sides. "We hear you're poking around the murder case down at the pier."

I sighed dramatically. "The same day, and already we're found out."

"This is the police's case, and you stay away from it," the brown-haired one said, still eyeing Brindos.

"Not so easy," I said. "We were hired."

"Consider yourself unhired," Bald Man said.

"Doesn't work that way." I leaned against my desk. "Who are you?"

Bald Man took a step closer. A strong odor came off him, as if he'd not showered for days and done nothing but boozed and ate rich spicy foods. The room suddenly felt dark and small and claustrophobic.

"You don't get to know that," Brown Hair said. "But we know you."

I shrugged. "Mr. Popular."

"I was told you were a bit of a wise ass," Bald Man said.

"Glad not to disappoint. Who told you this?"

Bald Man said, "The case. You need to forget it. If you don't, we'll have to make you forget it."

Obviously these two clowns didn't know me. Or Brindos. But *someone* had told them a little about us.

Brindos—cynical, reckless, who-gives-a-shit Brindos—would rub these guys' noses on the floor just to see if they squeaked. Brindos was young, granted, but he had a mean streak that stirred him frothy like a jump slot in flux. He left their noses alone and leaned toward the file cabinet without files in it. He opened it, pulled out his blaster, and covered them.

While Bald Man and Brown Hair tried to make sense of Brindos casually getting the drop on them, I pulled my own blaster from my waistband. They backed up, surprised. For some reason, they hadn't expected this offensive. They tensed, and Brown Hair stared nervously at Brindos. Bald Man kept his eyes on me.

Brown Hair made a mistake and tried to pull his weapon on Brindos. Before it was halfway out of his coat, Brindos slid forward and kicked Brown Hair in the knee, hard. The big man screamed and dropped, face down, and Brindos stepped on his hand and relieved him of his weapon.

Brindos snorted, crouched, and put Brown Hair's blaster on the floor right next to his face. "Here," Brindos said, "try it again. I need the practice."

Brown Hair didn't reach for it.

It was Bald Man's turn, and he reached

for his own blaster. I whipped my blaster up and fired a quick pulse past his ear. He cringed, arms protectively covering his head. Before he could recover, I closed the distance and caught him full force in the temple with my blaster. He stumbled backward, taking forever to fall to the floor. When he did, he attempted to scramble back to his feet, but I landed a vicious kick to his solar plexus. The air went out of him, as well as the fight, and when he was firmly on his back, I put my foot on his neck. I pointed the blaster at his head.

Brindos picked up Brown Hair's blaster and chucked it into the file cabinet without files in it. Brown Hair remained face down, arms spread, and Brindos put his foot on the thug's back. What do you know? Brindos actually *was* rubbing the man's nose on the floor. I heard no squeaking.

I threw Bald Man's blaster to Brindos, and he stashed it in the file cabinet and closed it. "Alan, it looks like taking a case offered by a dead man seems to have kicked up some garbage." We had definitely struck a nerve with someone, and there weren't many *someones* who could know about us being on the case. That had to narrow the field.

Brindos said, "Stinky garbage, too."

Bald Man's eyes lost their uncertainty and he smirked. "You won't shoot us, so I guess we're at a standoff. Doesn't change our warning."

"Why do you think we won't shoot you?" I asked.

They said nothing. Right, young and inexperienced. They didn't know what to think.

"You planned to rough us up, and it didn't work out," I said. "We could shoot and no one would care. I'd have a good story to tell, too. I'm sure we'd find out who you were, and who you worked for."

"The miracles of modern technology," Brindos said. "Thanks, alien benefactors."

"I doubt you'll find anything," Bald Man said.

I took a stab at it. "A Helk named John Grosko."

Brown Hair made a jerky motion with his head toward Bald Man, obviously taken aback, and Bald Man shot him an angry glance.

Ah, name recognition. It was time to press the issue. "Names," I demanded. "*Now*."

"Fuck you," Bald Man mumbled, the words barely a whisper due to the pressure on his throat.

"I know you know John Grosko. He killed my client." Now I just needed proof. Finding Grosko's body would be nice. I kept after him. "Your partner over there recognized the name. His reaction gave him away."

He swore at me again.

I put more pressure on his throat. "You work for Abigail Graff?"

"Who's that?" Bald Man wheezed.

"How about Brenden Thorne?"

"Who's that?"

He might be bluffing, but then again, the two of them could simply be muscle, hired to give us a scare. I let all that slide and tried another angle. "Okay, never mind. Tell me this. If I hypothetically needed a little something dreamy, a drug from Helkland, would you know where I could get it?"

Bald Man didn't answer, but he narrowed his eyes.

I raised my foot off his neck and placed it on his chest. Not too hard, just a firm pressure, reminding him I still had the upper hand. Or upper foot. "RuBy." I waved the blaster for effect. "You know where I can score some?"

Bald Man massaged his neck with his left hand. "I know about it. You can't get it here."

"Where'd *you* get it then?" I asked.

"Me? I don't touch the stuff."

"You both do."

"You're crazy."

No, I wasn't. I'd been at Thorne's crime

scene. The RuBy in his throat, and the smell. The overwhelming stench of stale food, but something sweet about it, like old pastries. These guys also smelled of that rich, cloying odor, which I at first attributed to bad hygiene, bad booze, and even worse food.

"Check his pockets," I told Brindos. Brown Hair seemed the easier target.

Brindos kicked Brown Hair roughly. "Roll over." The man did, pulling his injured knee toward him. "I can search—and I'm a little rough with that sort of thing—or you can show me yourself."

"Show you what?"

"The RuBy," Brindos said.

Brown Hair let out an exasperated sigh and reached into his black coat. When he withdrew his hand, he held a square of the drug.

Brindos took it and rubbed it between his fingers. "It's flimsy. Almost nothing." He sniffed at it. "Smells like cinnamon."

"Where'd you get it?" I asked.

"Don't talk," Bald Man warned.

Brindos bent down and thumped Brown Hair on the top of the head with his blaster. "You *do* know where."

"I can't—"

"Mr. Crowell here gets some, you get some. You understand? Kickback to you, no credits needed."

Bald Man tried to roll toward his buddy. "Andrew, shut up."

I increased the pressure on my guy's chest and wiggled my blaster above his face. "Let *Andrew* speak, or my foot goes back on your throat, and my trigger finger slips a little. The blaster will do a number on an arm or leg."

The man named Andrew sat up, and Brindos allowed it. Andrew rubbed his head. "Grosko could get it."

"So you do know Grosko."

"Yeah." Andrew stared at Bald Head a moment, then shrunk from his partner's return glare.

"Grosko is dead," I said.

Andrew blinked hard, then his face screwed up in confusion. "The hell you say. Grosko? I thought it was Thorne who was dead."

"Him too."

"We just talked to him—"

"Andrew, for Christ's sake," Bald Man said, "shut the hell *up*."

"Andrew," Brindos said. "What's your partner's name?"

Bald Man jerked his head. "Don't—!"

"He's Jake."

Brindos smiled at Jake the way a vulture looked at prey. Then he turned that smile on Andrew. "So," Brindos said. "The RuBy?"

Andrew kept rubbing his knee. "The TWT guy could get it. Grosko used him to deliver. That was it, I fucking swear."

My turn. "And where'd *Grosko* get it?" I motioned for Jake to sit up, and he did. "Answer the question, Jake."

He growled at me like a dog warning

someone away from his meal, then turned to his partner. "Andrew, you asshole."

"You said my name first, Jake," Andrew snarled.

I was getting very impatient with these two. "Jake. Where'd Grosko get it?"

"How should I know? We use it once in a while. The stuff's like acid, man. You have to be careful. If you don't pay attention, you end up with even worse shit. The experimental failures, the ones they discard. Someone gets hold of them and sells them and that's it, you're dead."

"Who hired you?" I said.

"I don't know. We thought it was Grosko. Just got pings. He said we do this, get you to back away, he'll get us the good RuBy. He said we don't do it, we end up like Thorne. He said he had connections. Resources. Above the law."

No one was above the law.

Mystery guy with connections. The case was beginning to coalesce and gel like those partially ingested RuBy squares.

"How did you know he was Grosko and not someone else?"

"Just by what he says in his pings," Jake said. "How he says them."

"So you're not sure."

This was my train of thought: John Grosko was a Helk with off-the-books passage to Helkunntanas, thanks to the inside work of Brenden Thorne. Thorne pays hush money to Abigail Graff. Graff hires Grosko to kill Thorne and keep her name clear. But this mystery person kills Grosko before he can do his job, and then kills Thorne anyway. But Thorne has already sent the delayed ping accusing Grosko of murdering him. When I stumble onto the case—literally, during my morning run—mystery guy promises these two idiots more RuBy to get me out of it.

But why? I was missing something. Mystery person kills both Grosko and Thorne. For what reason? For whose benefit?

Himself?

Connections.

"Grosko give you any instructions on how to get in touch with him?"

"No. He pings me."

"You hear his voice?"

"No. Unregistered."

"But it was coming from here. On Earth."

"Yeah." Jake was sullen, but cooperative now. We had him cold, even without possession of the RuBy, which was slightly illegal here.

I snapped my fingers at him. "Comm card."

"Ah shit, you don't need—"

"Comm card *now.*"

Jake dug it out of his black coat and handed it to me, his face turning scarlet; whether from anger or embarrassment, I couldn't tell.

Jake's comm card in one hand, blaster in the other, I spoke to Andrew. "Come over here, sit down next to Jake, back to back, hands behind you." Andrew didn't argue. While I rummaged through my desk drawer for bonding cuffs, he stood, tested his knee a moment, and hobbled over. He sat down and I put the cuffs on Andrew's wrists, then Jake's. They automatically cinched tight. He looked up at me and glared. I pointed a finger at him as if he were a disobedient dog. "Stay."

"What's next?" Brindos asked.

I threw the comm card to him and he caught it easily. "Do your magic. I want to know where that unregistered ping is coming from."

"Easy."

"If you can't work it out, I'll get detective McCoy on it."

Brindos gave me a hurt look—he didn't expect to need McCoy's help. He took the card to the DataNet terminal at my desk, and as he prepped the card, I dug out the virt tab McCoy had given me and rested it on the flashpaper of my own comm card. I expanded the surface and wrapped it around the tab to make the connection.

Once again, Alan Brindos's tech savvy came in handy. He'd found a way to break the proprietary lock on our comm card flashpaper so he could install a node to control a DataNet basement prog typically usable only in Authority comm cards and the code cards of the National Intelligence Organization.

The connection now enabled, the files of John Grosko filtered into the flashpaper and took hold. After the transfer, I removed the virt tab and expanded the comm card's flashpaper surface and saw all the files listed there neatly. I scrolled to the beginning and found tons of Grosko's personal data, including lists of known contacts, business-related and pleasure-related. The Helk had been busy on both sides.

I skipped through it and worked my way to McCoy's incident report. How she brought John Grosko in and held him for questioning. How she initiated the query log, compiled the embedded assessment and unofficial psych evaluation obtained from the holding room's scanners. Made a list of Seattle Authority personnel involved with all aspects of Grosko's time in detention. It even mentioned what they fed him for a day and a half, and how many credits it cost Authority before they turned him loose. Then a few days later, discovery of the body in a ditch out by an old farm south of the city. They brought it in, and dropped it off in the morgue. Then it disappeared, and the details of the entire affair never went public.

Jake and Andrew remained complacent, barely moving; the bonding cuffs hadn't constricted on them even once.

"Oh shit, no," Brindos said from the terminal.

"What? Source point?"

"Ping origination triangulated to Spring Street and 8th Avenue."

My heart sank when I heard the intersection. "Are you sure?"

Brindos nodded grimly.

"That's the old town hall," I said. "It takes up most of that block."

"It's not used much these days. Extra holding cells when needed, and overflow evidence lockers, but it's still the property of Seattle Authority."

Jake cleared his throat to get their attention. "That's right," he said. "Grosko—if it was him—said we shouldn't worry. He had the blessings of Authority, and the right to take you off the case. Said you had quit and compromised Authority's integrity."

I felt weak in the knees and had to sit down in the client chair. "Jesus. It's someone from Seattle Authority."

"Someone who's aware of you," Brindos said. "And if he's aware of you, he's aware of me, too."

"Give us protection from him and we'll tell you everything we know," Jake said.

"Yeah? What else do you know?" I leaned back into the chair and studied the virt tab's scrolling data.

Jake said nothing, and neither did Andrew.

"Yeah," I said. "They kept you in the dark as much as possible."

Brindos spoke up behind me. "Anything on the tab?"

I isolated the folders, flicked data away like annoying insects, and worked my way to the personnel file. "I can find out who else worked closely with Shirley McCoy on this. It's bound to be one of them."

"Dave," Brindos said, his voice low and reasoning. "You understand that it could be McCoy, right?"

"No." I refused to believe it. I stood and faced him. "She was my partner, and of all the cops there, the only one who still talks to me. She didn't do it."

"Probably not. But if you bring this forward, it'll be to her. You'll have to hope she's okay."

"She's okay."

I found the names and saved them as a separate node within the comm card's own file system. Once I tucked the flashpaper back, the virt tab's data would disappear. I glanced at the names more closely. McCoy, Sanderson, Bloom, Muller, and Pogosian, a DataNet specialist, and of course Captain Santos, whose name was appended to every report, regardless of his direct involvement.

"Sanderson and Bloom," I said.

"Those two were out there this morning," Brindos said.

A lot had already happened today. "Bloom flipped me off."

"Doesn't surprise me. Check the morgue scans?"

"Why?"

"To see if either of these two were at the morgue with John Grosko's corpse. The one that disappeared."

"That's a closed, secure system. You can't go in there without being seen or scanned."

"Unless you can disable the system."

"Not likely. Not those two."

"What about Pogosian?"

I laughed. "Even if she could, is she going to carry out a dead Helk? It would be nearly impossible for *any*one to get out of that building with Grosko, due to his size."

I found the report and whisked through it. There were entry logs, exit logs, holo-recordings, scans, and climate control readings. No coroner's report, no autopsy performed, the body disappearing before the coroner could do one. But definitely declared dead. "If someone disabled it, I certainly can't tell. Here's the day the body showed up missing. Nothing out of the ordinary that day. Assistant walks in, and the body's gone from its tray."

I studied the data, zipping through the files and recordings. If the mystery person killed Brenden Thorne, why did Thorne think Grosko was the one who would kill him?

Flick back to the day before. The day

they picked Grosko up. Nothing.

"Are we going to get protection?" Andrew said. His voice quavered a little.

"Shut up," Brindos said.

"Wait." I pulled a holo that showed a close full body scan of the victim. I let it run, zoomed, paused it, reversed it, and paused it again when Grosko's furry torso disappeared and his leathery head came into view. I pointed at a dark spot on the side of his neck. "What is that?"

Brindos stood and came around the desk. He took my card. After a few moments of study, he said, "It's an insignia."

"Of what?"

"It's a Helk thing. An employee badge grafted into the skin, for easy passage through the company's security."

"So it's a company he worked for?"

"Yeah."

"What's it say? What company?"

"It's in Helkunn. How should I know?"

Andrew spoke up. "Let me see it."

I frowned. "You know Helkunn?"

"Let me *see* it."

I took my card back from Brindos and brought it over to Andrew.

Andrew squinted at it a moment, then smiled. "Swain Dye-Works."

I looked at it again. "You sure?"

"I can't actually *read* Helk, but I know that logo."

The DataNet had mentioned a record of TWT payments to a dye-works in Swain. It would be one way Thorne could channel hush money to Abigail Graff. But if Thorne had been helping Graff and Grosko travel back and forth between Helkunntanas and Earth, why was *he* paying *them*? The money was backwards.

"How do you know the logo?" I asked. "How do you know this dye-works?"

"Because," Jake spoke up, "Grosko had us pay him for the RuBy through them. He pinged details about the credit transfer. It's a front."

"It's not a dye-works?"

"Well sure, it does business related to textiles and fabrics, but they're in on perfecting the red dye in RuBy. It's all hush hush, this company, and no one really knows who owns it."

"You still have the details he pinged you?"

Jake nodded.

That was it, then. Our John Grosko. It wasn't Brenden Thorne from TWT paying the Swain Dye-Works, it was these two assholes, and others, at the request of our mystery person. He killed John Grosko and somehow took over the back end of the dye-works business, pinging Grosko's contacts, staying in the shadows, no one realizing it wasn't really John Grosko. Jake and Andrew hadn't known Grosko was dead. The killer was channeling money paid to him by new RuBy addicts like Jake and Andrew, hiding it behind TWT, thanks to Brenden Thorne.

Thorne hadn't been paying hush money

to Graff. He was an addict too. I recalled Thorne's fingertips at the crime scene. Slightly red from using RuBy, and using more of it, obviously, than these two clods. When things went awry—when Thorne found out about the mystery person—he was killed. Killed in a brutally spectacular way to show "Grosko's" clients how much he meant business.

If John Grosko hadn't gone missing, the coroner might have found the Helk drug in his system and made the dye-works connection.

If we didn't solve this soon, John Grosko's body would show up at some grisly crime scene as another warning from the mystery man. Thorne had sent the delayed ping to us, but he didn't know Grosko was already dead. Like these two in my office, Thorne had believed it was Grosko, and believed Grosko was going to take him out.

The killer, a Seattle Authority cop, was using the department's resources to build a nest egg. Stepped into the RuBy trade, ready to make a killing. A killing different than the ones already made.

"I believe," I said, "it's time to give Shirley McCoy a call. We need to set a trap and find out who our mystery person is inside Authority."

Brindos nodded. "If you trust her, absolutely."

"I'll bring in Captain Santos, too."

"Bold move, considering he dislikes you."

"He loves McCoy, so he'll listen."

In the end, Jake and Andrew had given up the right information and, I thought, done it a bit too easily. I believed I knew why. I believed they themselves had been set up.

I pointed at them, bound together back to back on my floor. "We'll get these two protection."

There was an audible sigh of relief from Andrew. Jake nodded at me. "Thanks."

I finished, "After we use them for bait."

The next day around noon, Shirley McCoy and I sat at my favorite table at Zola's waiting for Monte Santos. Brindos had stayed at our office.

When Santos came in, he spotted us, ignored the server who greeted him, and walked back. Santos stared at me a long while when he reached the table. He was tall, lean, and didn't look happy. Then again, he never looked happy, a nearly permanent scowl the most prominent feature on his face. He took off his coat, placed it over his chair, and sat down. Still upset with me, I could tell, but he listened as I told my story. The anger on his face after he heard two of his detectives named as suspects told me he wouldn't stay mad at me for long.

Our server, Tod, knew Santos, and understood this was something he should stay out of. He brought water, a large thermos of coffee, and left us alone.

The killer was most likely Ralph Sanderson or Thomas Bloom, but I couldn't be sure. I couldn't rule out Amy Pogosian or Michelle Muller. Hell, I couldn't rule out McCoy, or even Santos. But in my mind, I *had* ruled them out. They were good cops, and I knew I could trust them.

Jake and Andrew would stay at Jake's place. I needed Santos to protect them with some heavy muscle—someone who was not a cop—while they waited for a ping. That wouldn't necessarily bring out the killer, who'd have someone else deliver the RuBy. If the ping came in, Jake would report that Brindos and I were off the case. If the ping didn't come, they would make a big payment to the dye-works via the credit transfer details, and that would get our killer's attention.

"And they've got that kind of credit to spend?" Santos said, his voice low and slow.

He had started sucking on a toothpick the moment he sat down.

"No," I said. "We'll need that from Authority. Quietly."

"Naturally. And what will you and Brindos do?"

"Search Sanderson's and Bloom's homes."

"Illegally, I assume."

"Never."

"Uh huh. You find something that connects one of them, great. The law says it's admissible in court. But there'd be a cost."

"Yeah, I know. Brindos and I would still face charges for the illegal searches."

"What about me?" McCoy asked.

"Look up their financials," I said.

"What am I looking for?"

"A money trail to Helkunntanas. Payments to Swain Dye-Works. Investment portfolios. Anything."

Monte Santos cleared his throat and pointed his toothpick at me. It was oddly unnerving. "I can get Luke Bellman to watch your guys."

"He's out of jail?"

Santos nodded, picking at his teeth again. "He's a good guy when he's not screwed up. He's a dead-eye with a weapon, big as a Fourth Clan Helk, and he's loaned his services to us before."

"Good. We don't want dead bait."

"Bloom and Sanderson should be out and about for me the rest of the day," Santos said, "and tomorrow, they're doing a swing shift, so there should be nobody home. I'll need the rest of the day to talk to Bellman, organize things quietly. We can do this tomorrow evening." He sucked on the toothpick some more, staring at me. He took it out, as if he were going to say something, then picked at his teeth again. Finally, he threw the toothpick on the table and stood. "You figured this out fast. One day after finding Thorne's body."

"Jake and Andrew forced the issue, and I think someone else forced them."

"But you thought it through. Everything sounds good." He pulled the coat off the chair. "This is why you're missed at Authority, Dave."

I kept my eyes on his. "Sorry."

He shrugged into the coat, fiddled with the collar, and pushed in his chair. "Don't be. Another year or two from now, you'll probably be doing something else."

"That is likely, considering how shitty private work pays."

"Something off world, maybe."

"Hell, no."

Santos nodded as he put his hands in the deep pockets of his coat. "McCoy, you good with all this?"

She frowned. "Why wouldn't I be?"

"You haven't had a partner for a while."

McCoy sipped at her coffee, then gave me a look I couldn't quite interpret, perhaps confusion, or admiration. I was leaning toward admiration.

"He's not my partner." She clicked my

coffee cup with hers. "But he's a friend. That works for me."

Santos actually cracked a smile. "Okay. Let's get to work."

We got to work. The next day saw preparations outside of the Authority building itself. Brindos drew Thomas Bloom's name. Bloom lived in a housing battery north of downtown in the old university district. I took Ralph Sanderson, who by chance lived a few blocks from Zola's in one of the nicer homes in the city. That right there told me a little, considering his Authority salary, because even after twenty years on the force, he'd be hard pressed to afford the place. McCoy pinged me with a brief on his financials, which included some offworld stock investments that, at least to her, seemed legit. She was still digging though, pulling what she could from the DataNet.

Santos loaned us skeleton key neutralizers to gain access and disrupt any alarms. I had my own access prog on my comm card, and didn't need his, but I took them, because mine didn't have the ability to take out an alarm, and it didn't have a flash panel status display. Plus, he didn't need to know I had *any* kind of skeleton key. Santos was right: if Brindos or I found something incriminating, we could use it in court. The times and the rules, they'd toughened up a lot in the last ten years. Santos might let us slide on the illegal search and avoid the one-year jail time. After all, he was the one loaning us the neutralizers to gain access. He'd be on the hook as well.

A little after four o'clock, at the same time Brindos approached Bloom's place, I slipped to the back of Sanderson's home, sprayed on my polymer gloves, and let the skeleton key do its work. The neutralizer's flash panel informed me Sanderson had an alarm, and a moment later, it was quickly rendered useless. The stat node registered me as the only life sign. I was alone.

The place definitely reeked of money. The front entry had high ceilings and a glossy redwood floor, and the place smelled fresh and clean. Past the entry was a spacious living room, and attached to that was a state-of-the art kitchen with more smart appliances than I'd seen in one spot before. I didn't rush things, but made steady progress through the house, staying vigilant, checking the stat node every few minutes.

I flicked an unfamiliar node to the right of the stat node and nothing happened that I could see, except that the skin of the node turned red and pulsed. I hoped I hadn't just called in the cavalry or something. That would be awkward.

I found Sanderson's study, which seemed a likely place to find a real life clue. Posh, like the rest of the house. Deep brown carpet, mahogany desk with a leather top, a gigantic original Sturgeon holo-enhanced metal painting on the wall behind the desk, and floor to ceiling bookshelves on the facing walls, boasting rows of paper books. Some of the books were old and rare volumes I ached to pick up and thumb through. Nothing was on the desk. The drawers yielded nothing.

So much for clues.

The upper floor was next. As I headed toward the main hall, I noticed paper peeking out from a space between two books on a smaller bookshelf to the left of the study door. I reached and pulled it from the gap and it was an actual paper photograph of Ralph Sanderson and two teenage kids, a boy and a girl.

But no.

He and his wife hadn't had kids, and she had left him for a lucrative job on Aryell selling vacation homes and arranging ski lodge rentals. On a hunch, I dropped the photograph on the shelf, face up, grabbed my comm card, and pulled up the data on Sanderson that Santos had pinged to me. I scrolled down Sanderson's personal file,

found my way to a list of known relation-
ships, and flipped through them like a man
whisking through personal ads on DataNet
holo-sites. Several dozen names came up.
Nothing. Then I worked my way to his
fellow Authority cops. About five names
in, the holo of Seattle Authority's DataNet
tech Amy Pogosian popped up.

I stared at the photograph. Amy looked
an awful lot like an older version of the
teenage girl in the photograph. Leaning
in closer, I noticed that the other teen-
ager, a boy, looked an awful lot like his
old man.

The year in the bottom right hand
corner gave me the context I needed. I
was looking at Sanderson's *father*. Ralph
Sanderson was the teenage boy, and Amy
Pogosian the teenage girl. Well now.
Brother and sister.

Pogosian the DataNet guru. She'd
figured out a way to doctor the records to
eliminate any connection to her and Sanderson. She'd tampered with the security

protocols so he could enter the morgue and do away with Grosko's body.

A call came into my comm card and I whisked the node. The flashpaper window filled with the stern face of Alan Brindos.

"Alan—" I said, but he cut me off before I could say any more.

"We've got him," Brindos said. "You were right about it being one of these Authority cops. Thomas Bloom's house smells like a cinnamon factory, and I found some stray squares of RuBy. And then McCoy called and told me about his payments. And then Santos called Bloom for an update on their case, and Bloom said his partner had run off because of a silent alarm."

"What? Brindos, slow down."

"McCoy didn't contact you? What about Santos?"

I looked down at my comm card and saw new message nodes. "Looks like I've got pings from them now."

"Bloom hid them pretty well, but the payments are to the Swain Dye-Works."

"Alan, listen. Goddamn it, we're *both* wrong."

"What are we wrong about?"

"I thought it was Sanderson. With help from Amy Pogosian."

"But it's Bloom. How am *I* wrong?"

"It was all *three* of them. And that false alarm report means they have some type of tracker prog that can snag the entry neutralizer's signal."

"So Bloom's coming here?"

"Did he have an alarm?"

"No."

A chill ran its way down my back. "Then no, he's not coming. Sanderson is coming to me."

"Are you sure?"

"You've got evidence for Bloom, but I've got the evidence—as subtle as it is— that ties Pogosian to Sanderson. Bloom is going to run at Jake and Andrew."

"Helk's breath."

"Have Santos arrest Pogosian. I'll have McCoy warn Luke Bellman that some-one's coming."

Brindos didn't bother with a goodbye. He blinked out. A moment later, I fumbled with the comm card in my left hand to bring up McCoy.

Precious minutes passed. C'mon, c'mon. Why wasn't she answering? Well, I hadn't answered her earlier, either. Or Santos.

As I flicked the message node from Santos, the hard barrel of a blaster jammed squarely into the back of my neck.

"Easy does it, Private Dick," came Ralph Sanderson's voice. "Just hand that comm card to me right now, if you please."

I swore under my breath and handed him the card. Moments later, I heard the telltale crack as he snapped it in half. He threw the pieces to a spot in the room where I could see them, just in case I hadn't figured out he'd broken the card. Then he rummaged in my coat, found my blaster, and took it. He thumped my shoulder with it, his own weapon still pressed against my neck. "Down. On your knees."

Down I went.

The pressure on my neck went away as Sanderson pulled the blaster away and came around to face me, both blasters pointed at me. Mine was DNA-locked, so he couldn't use it, but the sight of both barrels staring me down didn't make me feel any better.

Sanderson wore a dark blue sport coat over a gray button-down shirt, and his dark pants were immaculately clean and pressed. His swept back black hair had streaks of gray, and his face was wrinkled with worry lines. His pale blue eyes seemed to glimmer with amusement. He glanced at the photograph on the bookshelf and sighed. "You were on your comm as I entered the room, trying to get a hold of someone. Brindos, I assume. What've you got on me, Crowell?" he asked.

"Plenty."

"Elaborate please."

I returned his gesture he'd given me yesterday. "You're fucked."

"Because of this photograph? Please. Whatever you're thinking, you're jumping to conclusions."

"That's your dad. And you and Amy Pogosian as kids. Pogosian's your sister." If Sanderson had heard any of my conversation with Brindos, I hadn't said this revelation aloud, so the surprised look Sanderson gave me was priceless.

He tried to recover, but he wasn't convincing. "My sister. Really?"

"You worked together, because she could help with all the technical stuff. She hides the family connection. Alters the morgue security protocols. Bloom has the direct line to Helkunntanas and the Dye-Works. Maybe even Abby Graff."

"Jesus, Crowell—"

"You did the dirty work, defacing the Seattle pier with a brutal murder. No one on his own could carry a Helk's body from the morgue. But *together*, you and Bloom could do it. You took John Grosko's body from the morgue, and you hid it, because eventually the autopsy would show the RuBy in his system, connect it to the dye-works security mark on his neck, then back to Thorne, then to Jake and Andrew, then Bloom's payments. We've found RuBy squares in his home. Authority might even be able to trace the squares shoved down Brenden Thorne's throat."

Sanderson paled noticeably, but again, he did his best to recover. He forced a smile, nodded, and finally shrugged, keeping his shoulders up high for a long time. "That's good work, Crowell. But it's flimsy."

"That photograph connects a whole bunch of loose ends. Pogosian will crack, I'm sure. And if not, Authority goes looking, and finds the family tree eventually."

"Flimsy," he said, "because this photograph goes away in a puff of smoke with one good blaster hit."

"Then there's Jake and Andrew. You sent Bloom to get rid of them just before coming here."

Sanderson paused, weighing his response. "Even flimsier, then. I don't know how you finagled information from those two, but with them dead, you have no case. And who's going to believe you? McCoy? Sure, maybe. How are you going to get High and Mighty Monte Santos to buy in to it?"

I nodded. "Oh, you're probably right. You killed John Grosko, took over his trade, and you killed Thorne, and what can a private investigator find out that Authority can't? Particularly if you're controlling the information, and Pogosian's excising files and altering records."

Sanderson smiled, and it was not forced now. He thought he had me cold.

"You didn't expect Authority to find John Grosko's body," I said.

"I didn't, but all that got taken care of. I'll make an example of him just as I did

Thorne. You can't be soft when dealing with the districts on Helkunntanas."

"Why kill Thorne? He was a user. What threat was he to you?" I knew the answer to this, but I needed him to talk.

"He knew about the dye-works. He knew about Graff. He knew about Grosko."

"And he found out about you."

"No."

"He found out that Grosko wasn't Grosko anymore. It was *you*, but Thorne didn't know that. But he knew enough to expose you."

"Killing him was the only way to be sure, and leave a good message to John Grosko's clientele."

He waved his blaster at me, bringing my attention to it. He still held my blaster on me, too. He was a cop and knew it was DNA-locked, but he kept pointing it at me for effect.

Sanderson announced, "This will incinerate the photo in an instant."

"And then I'm next."

"That's right. You know too much, of course. Besides, you deserve it for bailing on Authority."

"Like you actually give a shit about Authority."

"You'll be dead long before anyone can save you," he said, ignoring that. "Even Brindos. If he's at Bloom's place, he's too far away. If we have to, we confess to illegal drug running. But that's it."

"Give it up, Ralph. You're not thinking straight. Santos already knows. He's in on this operation. He's got Bloom covered, and your RuBy boys protected."

"You're lying. Santos would never listen to you."

"I'm willing to bet it was Abigail Graff who set you up with the RuBy Boys. They were awfully forthcoming with information once we goaded it out of them. Graff, totally untouchable, needed to get you out of her way. She's got big plans on Helkunntanas, doesn't she?"

"Maybe. It doesn't matter." With his left hand, he pointed his blaster at the photograph on the bookshelf.

I made a decision. I leaned forward, got my legs under me, and rose awkwardly. I was stiff from kneeling, but it only took a few seconds to get to my feet and rush his right side, which was the moment when he triggered his weapon at the photograph. My sights were set on the arm holding my blaster.

As I'd hoped, he tried to shoot me with it. His own blaster had discharged, but nothing happened when he pulled the trigger of my own blaster. A split second later, he realized what he'd done. I collided with him, and we fell. Sanderson lost both blasters.

I hit the carpet hard. But it was a thick carpet, and I recovered quickly. I rose up, back to my knees, searching for my blaster.

There. I spotted it behind Sanderson's head. He lay on the ground, his eyes unfocused, but he quickly regained his senses. He turned his head. His own blaster was next to him, just within reach.

I dove for mine, a desperate chance. The feel of its familiar metal against my fingertips as I rolled past was like a moment of desperation, a last clawing at a branch of a tree to keep from plummeting to the ground.

My fingers curled around it, and as I found the grip and trigger, my roll finished. I was on my side, facing Sanderson. He had his own blaster, and he turned his head toward me, his face etched with rage. He saw me and tried to react, but before he could point and shoot, I fired.

The shot clipped his shoulder, disintegrating the fabric of his jacket. He groaned and swore. The second blast missed completely. The third hit true, charring his upper torso. Lucky shot, considering my position on the floor, and very little time to aim.

Sanderson stopped moving. Whether

he was unconscious or dead, I couldn't tell, so I rolled to my stomach and, with both hands, leveled the blaster at his head for several minutes.

Eventually, I stood and stared down at him. The fabric of his jacket sizzled like a sputtering firework, right near his heart.

He was alive, but barely. I took his blaster. He wasn't going anywhere, and if he died, he died.

My comm card was busted.

The photograph, unfortunately, had disintegrated into ash from Sanderson's blaster fire. It didn't matter. I had enough on him. I sat down in Sanderson's desk chair and waited for someone to arrive.

Fifteen minutes later, someone entered Sanderson's house and worked through the various rooms. The house was quiet, and I could track the someone fairly easily. I kept my blaster ready.

Shirley McCoy entered the room warily, her own blaster up. She scanned the first corner, turned quickly, and saw me sitting at the desk.

She noticed Sanderson next. She put him in bonding cuffs, but he still didn't move. If he didn't get help soon, he probably would die. She called Authority, raised Santos to tell him what was going on, and ordered an ambulance.

No one had warned Luke Bellman, but it hadn't mattered. Bellman dealt with Thomas Bloom fairly easily, incapacitating him when he showed up to kill Jake and Andrew. McCoy figured Santos would clear the two thugs in exchange for whatever information they could give Authority about John Grosko's operation.

Amy Pogosian was in custody, waiting for her lawyer. She hadn't said anything.

"You hurt at all?" McCoy asked.

I hadn't moved from Sanderson's desk. We were waiting for the ambulance and Santos. Night had fallen, and the black sky peeked through Sanderson's study window. "No, Shirl. I'm fine."

"Ambulance will get here soon. Authority should be right behind them." She sighed, staring down at Sanderson. "I hadn't considered all three of them could be involved.

"Neither had I. Until the photograph."

"And now it's gone. If Sanderson lives, and Pogosian doesn't talk, there's a chance the case will die." The idea of Sanderson getting away with murder filled McCoy's eyes with anger.

I shook my head. "He won't get away with it."

"Your testimony will help, but—"

I reached into my coat pocket and pulled out the skeleton key I'd used to enter the house and check my status. I slid it across the desk to her. "A present."

"A present?" She reached across and picked it up. "We gave this to *you.*"

"When Sanderson asked for my comm card, he took it and broke it in half, but I'd had the skeleton key in my other hand. He'd already searched my jacket pockets for my blaster, so I slid it back in there when he came around to face me."

"Okay, so?"

"The whole conversation's recorded."

She paused, confusion lining her forehead. Then I saw hope in her eyes. "Recorded. How did that happen?"

"I inadvertently set the record mode. Little node to the side of the stat display that turned red and started pulsing. I didn't know what it was. I only figured it out while waiting for you. I remembered the red node, activated it, and heard the recording. It has all the visuals too, up until the time I put it in my coat pocket."

Shirley McCoy grinned from ear to ear. "Good work."

"Lucky, I guess."

"Your middle name." She held the skeleton key with both hands, as if it were a fragile relic. "Looks like you earned your pay."

I'd almost forgotten about the credits Brenden Thorne had deposited into my account. "It's tough to come out on top and realize you still have a dead client."

"It was a brutal way for him to die."

"That RuBy is dangerous stuff," I said. Sure, the impaling had been horrific, but the potentiality of the alien drug and its ability to do harm on a Union scale screamed out at me like a warning beacon. "I'm not sure where that's headed, but it can't be good."

"We'll work on it. Get the word out."

I nodded, and the question I'd expected her to ask came up.

"Santos likes what you did on this case, Dave. Me too. Ever think you might return to Authority?"

Return to Authority? Sometimes the idea intrigued me. How long would this private work last, anyway? I *wanted* it to last, but I could easily see myself doing something different if I had to. The Union could spiral out of control tomorrow, and I'd be running somewhere else, looking over my shoulder, wondering what I was really up against and who to trust. The inevitability of change balanced precariously on a thin unstable line.

Return to Authority?

"Not a chance," I said.

Strobed light washed through the study windows. The ambulance had arrived. The colors flickered and ghosted across McCoy's face and the back wall, alternating between soothing pale blue and angry crimson.

About the Author

Patrick Swenson edited *Talebones* magazine for 14 years, from 1995 until 2009. A graduate of Clarion West, he's the author of the novels *The Ultra Thin Man* and the sequel *The Ultra Big Sleep,* and he has sold stories to the anthology *Like Water for Quarks*, and magazines such as *Marion Zimmer Bradley's Fantasy Magazine*, *Figment*, and others. He runs the Rainforest Writers Village retreat every spring at Lake Quinault, Washington. He is a high school teacher and lives in Bonney Lake, Washington with his son Orion.

OTHER TITLES FROM FAIRWOOD PRESS